The jungle became black as night as the storm worsened and the rain beat down. Every few minutes, blinding flashes of lightning streaked down from the terrible dark sky. Ground-shaking thunder followed moments later.

Suddenly after the rumble of some heavy thunder, Hank heard another sound. *That wasn't thunder,* he thought. *It's more of a roar than a rumble.* The roaring sound echoed again through the jungle. Then a bolt of lightning followed, lighting up the scene.

Hank gasped! Right before his disbelieving eyes, a huge creature emerged from the jungle into the open. Hank's mouth went dry and he found it hard to breathe. He fell to the ground in shock and pure terror.

Standing on its powerful hind legs, the creature looked like pictures Hank had seen of a tyrannosaurus rex!

Land of the LOST DINOSAURS

by Walt Oleksy

**Cover illustration
by Richard Kriegler**

*To Nick and Quinn McCumber
and
Kristen and Tina Lamberis*

Published by Worthington Press
10100 SBF Drive, Pinellas Park, Florida 34666

Printed in the United States of America

10 9 8 7 6 5 4 3 2 1

ISBN 0-87406-524-0

CHAPTER ONE
Over the Congo

Hank Cooper glanced nervously out of the airplane window at the ground swaying back and forth below him. He wiped his brow. The air in the old single-engine prop plane that he and his parents were flying in was thick with humidity. And the heat was stifling.

The plane shook from side to side, throwing the passengers back and forth in their seats, and then it leveled itself in the air. Hank took a deep breath and pulled his Chicago Bears cap down around his ears.

Above the rattly roar of the engines, Hank could hear his father arguing with the pilot, a tall, dark-skinned native who had introduced himself as Raymond Watana.

"The Congo is no place for a boy!" Watana was saying. "When you hired me for this trip, you said nothing about a boy and a wife."

"Why in heaven's name should it make a

difference?" Jeff Cooper spat back. "I booked a flight for three people and you've got three people in three seats."

"It makes a difference, Mr. Cooper," Watana said. "The Congo is a dangerous place. And the land beyond the Zoraba Mountains, where you have asked me to take you, is far into the jungle. Very remote. I can't be responsible for what happens to you out there—especially the boy."

Hank sighed. He was tired of being called a boy. After all, he was thirteen—barely a boy anymore. And his parents had been taking him on their archaeological expeditions every summer since he could remember. And it was a good thing he had been along last summer. If it hadn't been for him, his parents might still be in Bolivia—without their heads! Hank was the one who had saved his parents from headhunters!

"Hank is not a child. And it is none of your concern," Hank's father said sternly.

Hank's mother reached from behind Hank, put her hand on his shoulder, and squeezed it.

"Tell me, Mr. Cooper, what is it you search for in the land beyond the mountains?"

Hank turned to look at the other passenger in the plane, a tall, blond Australian man who wore a safari-style hat. He had introduced himself earlier as Paul Ruffington.

"We're going on an expedition to search for a lost city," Hank answered for his father.

Hank's father smiled broadly at Hank.

"We're archaeologists," Hank's father explained. "We are looking for evidence of the Zoraba civilization. They have quite a reputation in the Congo—idol worship, secret ceremonies, human sacrifices."

Hank broke in again. "There are some people who think that the Zoraba tribe still exists."

Hank's mother, Julie, sighed. "Hank, you know as well as I do that the tribe died out in the 1800s."

"And why do *you* visit the land beyond the mountains, Mr. Ruffington?" Julie asked.

"Call me Paul," Mr. Ruffington said with a smile. "I too am studying a civilization that died out years ago."

"Are you an archaeologist?" Hank asked.

"I'm part archaeologist, I guess," Paul answered. "I study dinosaurs—living dinosaurs."

Living dinosaurs? Hank pondered the idea for a minute. When he was a little boy, he had been crazy about dinosaurs. He had even wondered what it would have been like to have

7

a dinosaur live in his backyard. But even then he knew that dinosaurs had died out years and years ago. Living dinosaurs—impossible!

"You speak of *Mokele-Mbembe*," Watana said ominously from the front of the plane.

"You know the Mokele-Mbembe?" Paul asked anxiously.

"To speak of the Mokele-Mbembe is to invite their terror."

"Come now, Watana. You don't believe that the Mokele-Mbembe are really dinosaurs, do you?" Hank's father broke in. "That's impossible."

"Not impossible," Paul Ruffington said. "There have been reports of giant lizards beyond the mountains. In fact, there are rumors that these giant lizards wiped out the Zoraba tribe."

"But how could that be?" Hank asked. "Whatever killed the dinosaurs way back then killed them all. Some people think it was the Ice Age."

"I'm willing to believe that there were some dinosaurs that stayed alive—somewhere on this planet. Perhaps there was one region of the earth that stayed warm, in spite of the Ice Age. And, since we don't know exactly what killed the dinosaurs, how can we know that there aren't any still alive somewhere?"

Watana huffed from the front of the plane. "Only fools hunt for the Mokele-Mbembe. They are not plant-eating dinosaurs. They are terrible, man-eating lizards. It is why visiting the valley beyond the mountains should be forbidden."

"I think we can handle these so-called dinosaurs, Watana," Hank's father broke in.

"Ahh," said Watana, with an evil smile. "You can handle Mokele-Mbembe. But there are other dangers. Snakes. Killer ants."

Hank looked at the dense jungle below him and thought about what Watana was saying. Snakes, killer ants—they weren't exactly the kinds of creatures that hung out in his backyard in Chicago. But Hank and his parents were used to facing the wild—and they knew how to be careful.

The dinosaurs—the Mokele-Mbembe. They were something entirely different. But the stories of the living dinosaurs sounded like legends—like the stories he had heard about Bigfoot or the Abominable Snowman, the Yeti. Sure, they might exist, and Hank liked to think that they did, but they just didn't sound dangerous or threatening—just interesting.

Watana was continuing on about the dangers they would face.

9

"If you are lucky enough to get a guide to take you to the mountains, you must travel by river."

"Not a problem, Watana. Unless *you* get seasick, Paul."

"No—I'm at home on the water," Paul said.

"But this is no ordinary river," Watana argued. "There are places on the river with dangerous rapids and rocks. The natives call the worst of them the Gates of Terror. You must pass through them to reach the mountains," Watana said ominously. "And then, if you are very lucky, you will reach the land of the Zoraba. But, I tell you this, Mr. Cooper. I know of no one who has ever returned from there."

Hank thought for a second about what Watana was saying. Watana seemed to be making things up as he went along—inventing more and more reasons that he and his parents and Paul should stay away from the Zoraba valley. It was almost like he was trying to scare them away. But why?

Hank's thoughts were quickly interrupted when the plane bounced upward as if its underside had hit something hard. And then it started bumping up and down again and Hank began to panic. He could handle the jungle—but he didn't want to die in a plane wreck before he even got there.

"What's going on?" Hank asked Watana.

"Turbulence. This old plane can't handle the winds around here. The natives call them 'The Devil's Winds.'"

"Look!" Hank said, pointing out the plane's window. Below was a small village alongside a long and winding river. About a dozen huts with straw roofs extended up the riverbank.

"It is Mzadi," Watana said. "We will land here. Hold on to your seats."

The plane bounced and skidded on the rocky runway and finally pulled to a stop. Hank scurried to the front of the plane and pulled open the door.

When he stepped outside, he was immediately surrounded by tall, thin natives, dressed in colorful clothes. They called out in a language Hank couldn't understand. In the background, a half dozen dogs barked and yelped.

Watana began unloading, handing down their luggage to Hank and his parents and Paul, who had just climbed off the plane. One native boy came forward to help them with their packs—a boy about Hank's age. His black, braided hair hung down to his shoulders. He was shirtless, but he wore a pair of long, orange satin basketball warm-up pants.

11

Hank thought the boy was tall enough to be a terrific basketball player, but Mzadi didn't look like the kind of place that would have a basketball court.

"A man named Jerome Hudson is supposed to meet us here," Jeff said to Wantana. "Do you know him?"

"Looking for me?" a voice asked from the shadows. Hank turned and saw a young white man approaching. He was thin, with thick, blond hair and a mustache. Hank thought the stranger looked weird dressed in white slacks and a thin, silky shirt. He certainly wasn't dressed for a safari in the Congo.

"Hudson?" Jeff Cooper asked.

"Yes," the young man replied, extending his hand. "I'm frightfully sorry I wasn't here to help you unload your things."

Paul Ruffington stepped out from under the wing of the plane. "Ah, Jerome! How long it has been!"

Hank watched as the color drained from Jerome Hudson's face.

"Ruffington, yes," Jerome Hudson said, wiping his hands nervously on his pants. "Fancy meeting you here."

"Fancy, indeed," Paul said sarcastically.

Jerome Hudson turned abruptly and signaled for Hank and his parents to follow him. A million questions were running through Hank's mind—how did Paul know Jerome—and why did Jerome act so nervous around Paul? But they were questions Hank didn't dare ask as he and his parents followed Hudson along the riverbank.

After a few minutes, Hank saw the bamboo and straw house hidden among some trees. Hank followed his parents and Jerome Hudson onto the screened porch. The native boy followed with their gear.

"So, Hudson," Hank's dad began after they were all inside. "You know our new friend Paul Ruffington. What a coincidence."

"Not much of a coincidence really. There aren't many non-natives in these parts. We all seem to know each other," Hudson said nervously.

"I suppose that's so," replied Hank's dad.

The voices around Hank faded out as he looked around the inside of the straw and bamboo hut. From the outside, it had looked just like the native huts he'd seen in the village. But on the inside, it looked like a luxury apartment. The walls were covered with a thick brocade material. A velvet-covered sofa sat in the middle of the room. And on the walls were lots and lots of pictures. Hank moved from picture to picture. The native boy, who had dropped their luggage in the corner, was right behind him. Most of the pictures were of exotic places—the Taj Mahal or the Egyptian pyramids. One picture, though, stood out. It was a crude, native drawing of a huge lizard. And, at the lizard's feet, a young native boy was hurling a spear. Hank pointed to the picture and said to his native companion, "dinosaur?"

The young boy's eyes got big with fear. "Mokele-Mbembe! Mokele-Mbembe!" he shouted, and ran from the hut.

"They all have that reaction," Hudson said, breaking into Hank's thoughts. "The natives are terribly afraid of Mokele-Mbembe." Hudson wiped his brow on his sleeve. "I'm afraid I'm even having trouble finding porters for the expedition. So far, only two have agreed to go. The others are afraid."

"Are there really dinosaurs in the valley beyond the mountains, Mr. Hudson?" Hank asked.

"According to the natives, there are," Hudson said. "They claim that the dinosaurs leave the swamp to hunt along the riverbanks. They have been known to attack and kill people canoeing on the rivers. Then they disappear by digging cavelike hideaways in the banks. It's no wonder the natives are afraid

14

to take anyone on safari north of here."

"Have you ever seen a Mokele-Mbembe?" Hank asked Hudson.

"No, I've only heard stories," Hudson answered. "But frankly, I believe what I hear. Which brings me to another point—and I'm afraid you're not going to like it."

Julie Cooper shook her head. "It seems as if this expedition is doomed before it starts. What is it now, Jerome?"

"I won't be able to be your guide after all," Hudson said.

"Why not?" Jeff asked.

"Some urgent business has come up. It's unavoidable. I'm terribly sorry," Hudson answered. "Now, if I were you, I'd return to Brazzaville before dark. It's too dangerous to cross the mountains without a guide."

"You mean because of the dinosaurs?" Hank asked.

"There are also flying beetles, army ants, and gorillas," Hudson answered.

"It won't be an easy trip," Hudson said, "especially for the boy there."

Hank's father put his arm around Hank's shoulders. "Hudson, if it weren't for my son, Mrs. Cooper and I wouldn't be alive today. He goes wherever we do."

"Why don't you let me make the arrangements for you to go home? I'll get Watana and he can fly you out of here this afternoon," Hudson said, wiping more perspiration from his forehead.

What was Hudson keeping from them? He acted just like Watana had on the plane—it seemed he was making up more and more stories as he went along. *Why is he trying to scare us off and what is he trying to hide?* Hank wondered.

Hank swallowed hard when his father said, "We're going on with our plans. We start for the mountain tomorrow morning."

CHAPTER TWO
The Natives Are Restless

At dawn, the Cooper family was packed and ready to leave. Hank could hardly contain his excitement. As much as he knew that the stories about the dinosaurs were unbelievable, he couldn't stop thinking about it.

After Hudson had gone to sleep the night before, Hank's father had gone to the village and rounded up two porters. Apparently, Hudson hadn't tried very hard to convince the natives to accompany the Cooper family. The porters led the way, each carrying two backpacks. Hank and his parents followed single-file, each carrying a pack. The packs contained food, extra clothing, first-aid kits, and other essentials for the expedition.

Hank and his parents followed the porters up a path that ran along the Congo River. The porters began a sing-song chant as they walked. It was a low, soft, grunting sound.

They repeated it over and over. Hank found himself repeating the chant—it made the morning go more quickly.

When the sun was high in the sky, they stopped for a quick lunch and headed on into the jungle wilderness. After lunch, Hank began to have the strangest feeling. He felt as if someone was watching him. He kept looking in front of him, but he saw no one.

Except for some monkeys chattering in the trees every so often, the jungle was as quiet as a cemetery. Suddenly, the four porters stopped. Hank and his parents stopped, too. The porters talked anxiously among themselves and Hank wondered what they were saying. He could tell that his parents were wondering the same thing.

Just as suddenly, the porters stopped talking. They stood rigid and listened. Hank listened, too. All he could hear was the call of some birds somewhere deep in the jungle.

After listening intently for a few minutes, the porters threw off the packs they were carrying. They let them fall to the jungle floor. Waving their arms over their heads, they ran frantically into the jungle, then disappeared.

Hank just looked at his parents in disbelief. "Hey, what's going on with those guys? They looked really scared."

"Something horrible must have frightened them," Julie said.

A moment later, Hank's heart fell to his feet. He saw what had terrified the porters. Hidden in the leaves of the jungle, were half a dozen very tall natives, naked except for loincloths around their waists. Hank stifled a scream as he saw the face of one of the natives—it was hidden behind a hideous ram's-head mask. The rest of the natives stood half-hidden among the giant-leaved bushes and trees surrounding them. Their faces and arms were painted in stripes and circles.

They were lifting something to their mouths, but Hank couldn't see what they were at first. And then, too late, the sudden realization came to him—blowguns!

In an instant, Hank felt something hit his neck. He felt his knees buckle. The jungle began spinning around him, the calls of the monkeys echoing in his ears. The next sound he heard was the sound of his own body as it hit the jungle floor.

* * * * *

Hank was only vaguely aware of his surroundings. He felt awake, but every time he opened his eyes, it was as if something—some

19

force—forced them shut and he fell into a deep sleep again. He knew that night had passed. Once, when he opened his eyes, he had seen the moon in the sky. But where was he? And where were his parents? He opened his eyes once again, and was blinded by sunlight. It was daytime. He listened for voices, but heard only the chattering of some monkeys in the trees.

Then he heard someone—or something—and he forced his eyes open. He tried to bring himself to his knees so that he could run—but as he sat up, the sky began twirling around him. Hank fell back to the ground.

Through squinted eyes, he saw the faint outline of something familiar. He recognized who was coming toward him when he saw the orange basketball warm-up pants. It was the tall boy he had seen back in Mzadi.

"You must be hungry," the boy said, holding out some fruit for Hank.

Hank tried to sit up again, but couldn't.

"Be slow about it," the native boy said. "The blowgun poison has not yet worn off."

Hank took the native's advice and propped himself up ever so slightly. Then he raised himself to a sitting position.

"My parents?" he managed to ask.

"I do not know where they are," the native

said. "Here, take some fruit. It will give you strength. Then we will talk of finding them."

Hank looked at the boy questioningly.

"The fruit is safe. You see, I am on your side. My father too has disappeared. The men with the blowguns have stolen him."

Hank took the fruit and brought it to his mouth. It tasted something like bananas and cantaloupe, but not quite. Whatever it was, it tasted good.

The native boy sat cross-legged and smiled, watching Hank gulp down the fruit.

"My name is Oko," the boy said, smiling and bowing humbly to Hank. "I remember from Mzadi that you are the one they called Hank."

Hank just nodded.

"My village is near here," Oko explained. "My people are a small but peaceful tribe. They are disappearing, by ones and twos. Two weeks ago, my father vanished. I am on a journey looking for him. That is why I went to Mzadi. That is why I braided my hair."

Hank wasn't sure he understood.

"I needed to disguise myself—so I braided my hair so that I would fit in with the natives of Mzadi," Oko explained. "I trust no one in the village or the jungle. Except, maybe, you."

"You don't know me," Hank said. "Why do you trust me?"

"You trust me, do you not?" Oko asked.

Hank nodded that he did. "I don't know why, but I do."

"Ah, then we trust each other," Oko said.

"Do you know anything about Jerome Hudson, the guy who was supposed to be our guide?" Hank asked.

"I never saw him before yesterday," Oko said.

"Hudson was supposed to take us up to the Zoraba Valley. Then when we met him at Mzadi, he made up some kind of excuse that he couldn't. He said the other men in the village were afraid to go up in the mountains."

"Everyone is afraid to go there," Oko said.

"Is it because of..." Hank stopped himself, remembering Oko's terror earlier. "...the, you know, the lizard things?"

"We do not talk of them. Perhaps they exist. Perhaps not. But to talk of them is bad luck."

Hank nodded his head and continued.

"Paul Ruffington—a man we met on the plane—was sure that they existed. He had even come here to study them."

"Many people come to study them—few return. Let's hope Mr. Ruffington is very careful."

"What about the Zoraba?" Hank asked. "They are supposed to live in the valley

beyond the mountains. My parents were..."
Hank hesitated as he thought about his
parents. They could be anywhere in this
jungle. They could be tortured, held captive,
or even dead. Hank could barely stand to
think about it.

"There are legends of the Zoraba. Some say
they still exist. They were a fierce people. And
they believed in the Mokele-Mbembe. It is
said that they practiced human sacrifice in
the hopes that the Mokele-Mbembe would not
bother them."

Hank finished his fruit and wiped his
mouth.

"My village is ahead," Oko said. "There is
not much to eat, but we will share food with
you. Then you must rest and I will tell you
my story. Maybe some of it fits with yours."

Hank was just bringing himself to a standing position when he heard a strange sound.

"Listen," he whispered to Oko.

It was a steady, low, rumbling sound.

"What is it?" Hank asked. "Where is it
coming from?"

"It sounds like it is coming from somewhere
over our heads," Oko said in a shaky voice.

"It's coming closer!" Hank shouted, as the
long, black shadow of a wing darkened their
path. "What if it's a Mokele-Mbembe?"

CHAPTER THREE
Danger in the Night

Trembling, Hank and Oko looked up toward the sky for the source of the shadow. They caught a glimpse of an airplane through the jungle trees.

"It's flying very low," Hank called to Oko above the noise. "I think it's going to land. But the landing strip at Mzadi is too small for a plane that big. What's it doing out here?"

"I do not know," Oko replied. "We have started seeing more and more planes like that one lately. Like the disappearance of my people, it is a mystery."

Then they heard the low, rumbling noise again.

"The plane is returning," Oko said.

"Look how low it's flying. It must have landed somewhere nearby, and then taken off again," Hank said. "I wonder where the landing strip is."

The boys walked in silence for a while. Hank thought about the cargo plane and whether or not it held a clue to his parents' where-abouts. As the sun dropped low in the sky, they arrived at Oko's village, a village made up of the same straw-roofed huts that Hank had seen in Mzadi—only fewer of them.

Some scrawny wild dogs were the first to greet them. One of the dogs came running up to Oko. The skinny, black mutt with gray streaks wagged his tail at Oko.

Oko scratched behind the dog's ears. "This one is mine," he said. "She is old now, but she was a puppy when I found her along the riverbank."

Oko bent down and let the dog lick his face.

"This is my friend, Hank," Oko said, intro-ducing them. The dog raised her head to let Hank pet her. "Her name is Nuzu," Oko said. "In our language, that means 'hungry.' You should have seen her eat when she was a puppy!"

Hank laughed. "What does 'Oko' mean?"

"Playful," his friend replied. "You should have seen me when I was very little."

"That reminds me," Hank said. "I noticed that you're wearing basketball warm-up pants. Are you on a team somewhere? Is there a school here or in Mzadi?"

"I have never gone to school, though it is my second greatest wish," Oko said. "My father got these pants for me, from Brazzaville. He played on a high school team there. He is the one who taught me English. He taught English to our whole tribe." Oko smiled proudly.

"You're tall enough to be a great basketball player," Hank said.

"It is my third greatest wish," Oko replied.

"So what's your first greatest wish?" Hank asked.

"To find my father alive again," Oko said as he began walking ahead. Hank followed Oko, the dogs prancing along behind him.

As they walked through the village, Hank saw only very young children and very old people.

"Where are the older kids and the parents?" Hank asked.

"They are the ones who have been disappearing," Oko replied. "It has become dangerous to stray very far from the village. Even those who take walks to the river have not been coming back."

"You mean they're being kidnapped?" Hank asked.

"We do not know what is happening," Oko said. "Our people just seem to vanish. We have never found their bodies."

Oko led Hank to a hut on the edge of the village. Then he called inside the open doorway. A moment later, a voice told them to enter.

As soon as they entered the one-room hut, Hank noticed a strong smell, like paint. It was so dark inside that Hank could hardly see. Once his eyes adjusted to the dark, he saw an old man lying on a cot, its metal legs standing in old cans.

"He is our shaman," Oko whispered to Hank. "Our holy man and medicine man."

Hank looked toward the man. His eyes were dim and he could barely lift his head. To Hank, he looked very ill.

"Djoni, I have brought a friend to meet you," Oko said to the man.

The man tried to stand up, but fell back down to his cot in exhaustion. Oko helped him to a sitting position.

Oko introduced his friend. Then he told Djoni in English what had happened to Hank and his parents.

"Do you have any idea why this is happening or who is doing this?" Hank asked Djoni.

"I do not know," Djoni said. "But I want you and Oko to vow that you will not rest until you learn who is taking our people."

"You can count on me," Hank replied.

"We will not stop until we find the enemies and our people are returned," Oko added.

"Then indeed you are friends," Djoni said, smiling weakly. "More than that, you are brothers!"

"Could the people who are doing the kidnapping be the Zoraba tribe?" Hank asked.

"I do not know," Djoni answered. "A few months ago, before our people began to disappear, I was on the river near the great waterfall. I saw a man wearing a ram's-head mask—a sign of power in the Zoraba tribe. He was on foot followed by some others carrying spears. They were leading some other natives toward the mountains."

Hank felt certain that his parents were being held somewhere near the mountains. He looked at Oko and could tell by the expression on his friend's face that they were sharing the same thoughts.

Djoni raised his hands to the boys as if in a blessing. "You must rest now. When the sun rises tomorrow, you will start for the mountains. If it is the Zoraba, their ancient lands are there," he said.

The old man lowered himself onto his bed. Oko took Hank by the arm and began to lead him to the door. They were both startled by the sight of someone standing in the open doorway.

The shirtless man was wearing old blue jeans. He looked tall and strong, but not very friendly.

"He is the shaman's son," Oko whispered to Hank.

"What are you doing here?" the man asked. "Can't you see my father is ill? Who is this boy, Oko? What is a stranger doing in camp?"

"He is my friend, Tongo," Oko explained. "He will do us no harm."

"How do we know that?" Tongo demanded. "Our people are disappearing. Your own father among them! Who knows who is stealing them? Where does the boy come from?"

Hank answered for himself, "We came here from America. My parents have disappeared, too..."

"We don't have enough for our own people to eat," Tongo said angrily. "We can't feed strangers. Oko, you will have to feed him out of your share."

Djoni spoke up from the cot in the corner. "The boy is our guest," he said weakly from his bed.

"Rest, my father," Tongo said. "I will look after the boy."

Tongo ushered the boys roughly out of the

hut. He squeezed Hank's arm so hard it hurt.

"What are we to do with you?" Tongo asked, looking at Hank.

"Let him rest here tonight," Oko said. "I will give him some of my food. In the morning, I will take him back to the river and show him the path that leads back to Mzadi."

"The sooner we're rid of strangers, the better," Tongo said.

After Tongo left them alone, Oko took Hank to the village well where they drank their fill of cool water. Then he led Hank to his hut.

As soon as they entered the hut, Hank noticed the same strong smell he had wondered about in the shaman's hut.

"What's that smell?" he asked. "It smells like paint or something."

"Kerosene," Oko replied.

"What do you use kerosene for?" Hank asked.

"To keep away the ants," Oko said.

Hank remembered what Watana had told him about the ants. "Army ants?"

"Yes. We have to be prepared for them, always," Oko said. "See our cots?"

Hank saw two cots next to each other in one corner of the room.

"Why are the cots' legs standing in cans?" Hank asked.

"We pour kerosene into the cans," Oko explained. "It's the only thing that will stop the ants. If they come marching into our huts while we're sleeping, the kerosene keeps them from crawling up the legs of our beds and eating us alive."

Hank shivered. He wasn't sure if he could sleep knowing that he might be attacked by army ants.

"We'll be sleeping here tonight," Oko said. "Don't worry. The kerosene works."

"I hope so," Hank said.

Oko reached into a pouch he was carrying and handed Hank some fruit.

"It's very good," Hank said. "What is it?"

"We call it landolphia," Oko replied. "Here, try some of this meat."

Hank tore into some strips of what tasted like dried beef, only more bitter. "What's this?" he asked.

"Dried gorilla meat," Oko said.

Hank nearly gagged. Then he remembered that Oko was sharing what little food he had with him and tried to swallow the tough meat.

"Then there are gorillas around here?" Hank asked, finishing the meat and taking more fruit.

"Oh, yes. They can be very mean, but not as mean as Tongo," Oko said, laughing.

"He scares me," Hank said.

"You are wise to be frightened," Oko said seriously. "He wants to be shaman, but cannot until his father dies," Oko said. "The waiting makes him anxious—and dangerous."

"I hate to say it, but it doesn't look like he has much longer to wait," Hank said.

"Djoni is very ill," Oko agreed.

Hank shook his head sadly and decided to change the subject. "So, what lies between here and the mountains?"

"Next we need to journey through the Gates of Terror."

"Have you ever canoed past the Gates of Terror before?" Hank asked.

"No," Oko said, then smiled. "But you Americans have a saying, don't you? 'There's a first time for everything!'"

Hank laughed.

"Now, we must sleep," Oko said. "We will need to be strong for tomorrow."

Oko offered Hank his father's cot to sleep on. Across the room Oko stretched out on his own cot. Nuzu came in the hut, wagging her tail. Then she climbed onto the cot with Oko and curled up at his feet.

Hank stretched out on his cot. He was so weary after the day's adventures, even the thought of army ants couldn't keep his eyes open. Before he knew it, he fell off to sleep.

During the dark of the night, the dog's growls awakened the boys. "What is it, Nuzu?" Oko asked, getting up.

Oko started for the door, but told Hank to remain in the hut. He would see what had disturbed his dog.

Hank was so tired, he fell off to sleep again without waiting for his friend to return.

Later, in a half-sleep, Hank felt someone put a hand over his mouth and his eyes. Unable to cry out for help, he tried in vain to struggle free. He felt himself being lifted off the cot and suddenly realized that he was being carried out of the hut!

CHAPTER FOUR
The Gates of Terror

Hank felt someone carry him into the bushes that surrounded the village. Then, he felt the hand remove itself from his mouth and eyes.

Hank struggled free and looked at his captor. He gasped.

His kidnapper was none other than Paul Ruffington. "Hey, what's the big idea?" Hank asked.

"Listen to me, Hank, just listen. I know where your parents are. I needed to tell you—but I couldn't risk showing my face in that village. They don't appreciate strangers. I have visited them before and did not receive a friendly welcome."

"Tongo?"

"He was the meanest of them all, but the village was full of those willing to do me in. They do not like anyone asking about the

Mokele-Mbembe. They say it is bad luck."

"So I've heard. But what about my parents? Where are they? How did you get here?"

"They have been kidnapped by natives who may be from the Zoraba tribe. I don't know. One wears a ram's-head mask and seems to be the leader."

"Why did they kidnap my parents? And why are they stealing people of this village? What's going on, Paul? I've got to know." Hank's voice was becoming louder and louder with each word he spoke.

"Shhh, Hank, we don't want to be discovered," Paul said in a whisper. "There is some project in the valley beyond the mountains. I don't know exactly what it is—it is a secret project. And that man Hudson has something to do with it. I knew he was no good that time I met him in South Africa. He was mixed up with Grayson Powers, an industrialist who cares nothing for Africa or the Congo! Powers cares only about making money. And the land—the earth—the environment—well, as far as Powers and Hudson are concerned, they mean nothing!"

"But what about the kidnappings?" Hank asked, interrupting Paul.

"The natives are being kidnapped into slavery to labor on the project."

35

"And my parents? Have they been sold into slavery?"

"Your parents have been kidnapped by the same people who are kidnapping the natives—but they aren't being sold into slavery. You see, I was kidnapped along with them. But I managed to escape. Their fate is far worse than slavery."

Hank swallowed hard. "Go on," he said, his voice rising again. "Go on!"

"It is said that they will be sacrificed to satisfy the Mokele-Mbembe."

"When?"

"The sacrifice will occur on the night of the next full moon—and that's only three days away!"

Hank's head was spinning from everything Paul said. He had a hard time believing that Paul was telling the truth—but it sounded logical enough. And why else would Paul risk so much to come here and warn him? Hank shuddered at the sudden realization that he had just three short days to find his parents. But could he trust this stranger?

"We have to head for the mountains. I'll go get Oko."

"I'll wait here," Paul said.

Hank headed through the bush toward the village. But when he got to the edge of the jungle that surrounded the village, he looked up to see Tongo blocking the way between him and Oko's tent.

"I see you are leaving," Tongo said. "You'd best be quick about it." Tongo was stroking the blade of a knife that he kept in a sheath on his belt.

"I just want to tell Oko that I'm going."

"No need to disturb Oko," Tongo said, pulling out the knife.

Hank's heart began pounding hard.

"It is best for you to leave, now!" Tongo said, raising the knife in the air.

Trembling, Hank turned and ran from the camp. As he ran, he kept saying over and over, "good-bye, Oko, good-bye, Oko."

Hank returned to the spot where Paul was waiting for him and the two of them silently made their way through the jungle. Once or twice, Hank thought about asking Paul if he had seen the Mokele-Mbembe since he had been in the jungle, but thought better of it. It was best to keep quiet. Their journey through the dense foliage made enough noise as it was.

After an hour or so, the jungle stopped at a long, wide river. The moon's glow made the river shimmer like diamonds. There was a long dugout canoe beached on the riverbank. Hank looked at Paul questioningly.

Paul shrugged his shoulders. He pulled some moss and vines off the canoe. "It looks abandoned."

Hank shrugged his shoulders back at Paul and they both climbed in and began paddling up river, into the heart of the jungle.

As the boat moved through the water, a million questions went through Hank's mind. Were his parents okay? Was Oko's father okay? And would Oko catch up with him? And then, just as suddenly as the other thoughts spun through Hank's mind, he thought of home. It seemed so far away. Did the Cubs win today? How was his neighborhood baseball team doing? Had the pool opened for the summer? Hank looked at the jungle around him and felt very small and very lonely. He felt like a kid and he just wanted to go home.

Hank and Paul paddled for what seemed like hours. Every once in a while they talked, mostly about Grayson Powers and whatever his project might be. Hank suggested that they just confront this Powers to find out where his parents were being kept. But Paul warned that Powers was a dangerous man. In South Africa, he had kidnapped natives to work in his power plant. And he had destroyed the jungle, land after land, until there was nothing left. Powers cared nothing for human life—or animal life—or nature at all, according to Paul. Still, Hank thought that if he could only talk to him, he could reason with him, convince him to let the natives, and his parents go free.

When the sun was just coming over the horizon, they pulled the canoe up on shore and hid the boat under the brush and rested for a bit. Hank was asleep before he knew it.

Hank was awakened by Paul's voice.

"Hey, sleepyhead," Paul was saying. "There are pancakes on the griddle—and hot bacon, and sausage, and orange juice..."

"Stop it!" Hank said, smiling. "It's driving me crazy just thinking about it.

Paul held up a melon-like fruit. "This is the next best thing."

Hank took a piece and ate hungrily. It wasn't like breakfasts at home, but it was good just the same.

Soon Hank and Paul were in the canoe again. As they paddled the boat in the hot morning sun, Hank began to hear a low, roaring sound.

It was coming from somewhere ahead of them. A strong wind began blowing over the river, churning up huge waves that battered the small canoe. Within a few minutes, Hank's clothes were soaking wet. From the front of the canoe, Hank looked back at Paul, who yelled over the roar—"It's the Gates of Terror, boy. Hold on to your hat!"

Hank's hands trembled on his paddle as he remembered what he had heard about the dangers of the Gates of Terror.

The waves grew higher, splashing inside the canoe and filling the floor with water.

"Just hold on!" Paul was yelling. "Just hold on! And keep paddling!" As Hank held on to one side of the canoe, he saw the river begin to narrow. Ahead was a series of rapids where white-capped waves crashed over rocks that jutted out from the water.

Above the narrows, Hank saw two huge rock cliffs. They stood like granite towers on either side of the river.

"The Gates of Terror!" Paul shouted from behind him.

The canoe shot forward uncontrollably. As it entered the narrow passageway, the canoe was tossed around like a leaf in the wind.

Hank gasped for breath.

The canoe shot skyward, with its nose out of the water. Hank saw that the rapids were dying out ahead. Beyond the deep hole in the river, the water looked more calm.

It was impossible to paddle. Hank just held

on to the side of the boat for dear life. Behind him, Paul was doing the same.

Suddenly, Hank felt the canoe land with a boom and then he heard a sickening sound— a loud crash and then a splintering. The boat had crashed into a wall of huge rocks that seemed to rise out of nowhere.

Hank felt himself being pushed underwater. Then he felt himself being hurled into the water. He thought about the advice that he'd been given on a raft trip in West Virginia he took once. Just relax, the guide had said. Don't fight the current.

Hank willed his body to go limp. The rapids forced him left, then right. Then they spun him around.

Finally, he surfaced in the calm pool he had seen upstream. Gasping for air, he looked around for Paul, but didn't see a sign of him. The pool was calm and empty except for some long, green logs that were lying at its edge.

As he got closer, Hank screamed. The green things he'd seen weren't logs—they were a pair of crocodiles! And they were headed his way!

CHAPTER FIVE
The Jaws of Death

Hank swam frantically for shore. He knew that if he looked behind him it would only waste time. Instead, he looked ahead to his destination—the shoreline.

As he swam, he tried not to imagine what might happen to him if the crocs caught up with him—but he couldn't help it. He thought about their wide mouths full of long, sharp teeth. He could almost feel those teeth snapping·at his feet. His arms became heavier and the shore looked farther and farther away. He dared look behind him and he saw just how close they were.

Hank panicked. They were so close he could almost feel their breath on him. He'd never beat the crocodiles to shore!

Hank needed help, but he knew he was on his own. He glanced over his shoulder and saw one of the crocs open its mouth, ready to bite.

Hank looked around in desperation. Then he saw it—a low vine hanging over the water. He wasn't sure he'd be able to reach it, but it was his only chance.

He reached up and grabbed hold of the vine. With all the strength left in him, he pulled himself up until he was just above the river.

Climbing hand-over-hand up the vine, Hank looked down to see the two crocodiles' jaws as they opened wide directly under him, then clamped shut again.

He wasn't sure that he could climb the vine fast enough. The crocodiles splashed around in the water beneath him, looking up at him with hungry eyes.

Suddenly, something flew past Hank's head. It brushed past his left ear, then bounced off his shoulder as it fell. He looked down to see the two crocodiles fighting over it.

It looked like some kind of small animal, maybe a monkey. Whatever it was, it was keeping the crocs busy, at least for the moment.

Now Hank had the precious seconds he needed. He scurried up the vine until he reached a branch strong enough to support him. It hung high enough over the water so the crocodiles couldn't get him.

He had made it to safety—but just barely. The crocs were finished with their snack and were looking up at him for their main course.

Hank rested for a few minutes and scanned the water for Paul. There was no sign of him, either in the river or on the other bank.

Then Hank saw it—Paul's safari hat was floating in the water. He sighed and shook his head. Paul hadn't made it—Hank knew that now. He squeezed his eyes shut and tried not to cry. But even though he tried very hard, he couldn't help allowing two teardrops to stream down his face.

But Hank didn't have much time to feel sorry for himself. The branch he was sitting on was creaking ever so slightly. He was afraid it might break and then he'd end up as the crocodiles' dessert. He scooted along the branch until he reached the tree, then he jumped to the ground.

As his feet hit the grass, the crocodiles snaked their way to shore. They followed him, but he had no trouble outrunning them. Finally, they gave up. He looked back to see them return to the river.

Hank looked around him. *What now?* He sat down on a rock and put his face in his hands. Then he clenched his fists and banged them hard against a nearby tree. He couldn't quite understand what he was feeling—it was part anger, part despair, but mostly, he felt lonely—terribly, awfully lonely. He rubbed his shoulders, trying to rub some warmth into his wet clothing. The jungle air was hot and muggy—but Hank was freezing.

"I've got to get a hold of myself," Hank said aloud to himself. "Think, Hank, there's got to be a way out of this."

Suddenly, Hank heard a roaring sound from within the jungle. His first thought was the Mokele-Mbembe. But it didn't really sound like a fierce roar. And it was steady, without a change in pitch. Hank was too far upstream to hear the sound of the rapids. But this sounded like water—and it was coming from somewhere in the jungle.

Hank jumped up and ran—ran without stopping, toward the roaring sound. It had to be a waterfall. And on the other side of the waterfall, was the Zoraba Valley and—although Hank only dared to hope it—his parents.

The dense undergrowth tore at Hank's legs, but he kept running anyway. Suddenly, he stopped. In front of him was the most awesome sight he had ever seen—a massive waterfall cut out of the jungle. Millions of pounds of water tumbled down rugged rocks. Hank was still a quarter of a mile or so from the falls, but he could already feel the mist in his face.

Hank's heart began to beat rapidly with hope. He had found the Zoraba Mountains all by himself.

But just as quickly as his hopes had risen, they were dashed again. Hank stared at the falls. They fell over steep walls of granite cliff. Hank walked closer to the waterfall's sides and shook his head. *No way,* he thought. *There is no way that I can climb these cliffs.*

Hank felt a sob rise in his throat as his knees buckled from exhaustion. He fell face down on the jungle floor and lost himself in the deep, black sleep of despair.

CHAPTER SIX
No Way Out

The next thing Hank felt was someone shaking him. He was back in his room, in Chicago, and it was time for school.

"Come on, Mom," Hank said. "Just let me sleep another couple of hours."

Hank felt someone shake him again. "Aw, Mom," Hank groaned. And then he shook himself from his dream and opened his eyes.

A blood-curdling scream echoed through the jungle. Hank held his throat when he realized that it came from his own mouth.

In front of his eyes was the most incredible sight he'd ever seen!

It was Oko! And next to him, his dog, Nuzu.

"Oh, Oko!" Hank said. "I never thought I would see you again. I tried to go back for you, but then Tongo..." Hank's words were tumbling out so fast now he could barely control them. "And Paul found a canoe and we made it through the Gates of Terror..." Hank paused, remembering what must have been Paul's fate. "At least...I made it. And then..."

"Slow down, my brother," Oko said, smiling. "I am just glad to find you safe. I have lost too many friends—I didn't want you to be the next one."

"Listen, Oko," Hank said, as if he hadn't even heard Oko's words. "I found out about my parents and your father. They're in the valley beyond the mountains. Your father is a slave, I think, on some special project. My parents..." Again, Hank paused, overcome with horrible thoughts. "My parents are going to be sacrificed to the Mokele-Mbembe."

"You mustn't speak of them!" Oko said. "It will bring bad luck. And besides, you have been in the jungle a long time now. Have you seen a Mokele-Mbembe?"

Hank shook his head sheepishly. "No, I haven't, but we haven't reached the valley yet." He looked up at the towering mountain and sighed. "And I don't know if we ever will."

"Don't be so sure, Hank," Oko said. "After all, we both made it through the Gates of Terror, didn't we?"

"Hey, that's right," Hank answered. "How'd you do it, Oko? How did you manage it by yourself? And where did you find a boat?"

"Djoni let me borrow one from the village. He braved the Gates of Terror many times in his youth. He told me how to avoid the worst of the rapids." Oko swept the back of his hand across his brow. "But it was not easy."

"Tell me about it!" Hank said, sighing.

"And climbing this mountain won't be easy, either," Oko continued. "But we can do it— we *must* do it."

"But how?"

"This might help," Oko said, pulling a rope with a grappling hook on it from the backpack he wore on his back.

Hank smiled at Oko. "It might—it just might." They both shot their eyes upward, looking for footholds or a place to anchor the rope.

"It looks like there is a ledge—see it, about halfway up," Oko said.

"Yeah, I see it," Hank said, squinting. "It's pretty high."

He smiled. "Well," he said. "We have nowhere to go but up!"

"Let's get started." Oko hurled the rope upward toward the rock ledge. The first throw brought the rope and its anchor tumbling back down. But the second throw anchored the rope—and when Oko tugged on the rope, he pronounced the anchor firm.

Then Nuzu started to whine.

"What do we do about Nuzu?" Hank asked.

"Nuzu," Oko said. "You must stay behind. You can wait for us here."

Nuzu's whine turned into a high-pitched growl. "You'll be okay, girl. And we will be back soon—I promise."

Nuzu didn't look convinced—and neither was Hank. But Oko was rubbing his hands in anticipation.

"I'll go first," Oko said.

Hank was in no mood to disagree.

Hank watched from the ground as Oko made his way up the side of the mountain toward the ledge. He took each step slowly, first making sure he had a foothold, and then moving his foot carefully to the next spot. Hank felt himself concentrate with each step, trying to memorize each foothold that Oko selected. Finally, after what seemed like hours, Oko reached the ledge.

"Okay," he shouted from above, "your turn!"

Hank took a deep breath and rubbed his hands together. Nuzu whined and looked at him questioningly.

"It's now or never, Nuzu," Hank said. He walked toward the rope and grabbed it with both hands. Slowly, he moved his feet against the mountain. The rocks crumbled beneath his feet and he lost his footing for a second. But he tried again, concentrating hard, his hands white against the rope. He thought about gym class, and shimmying up the rope to the gym ceiling. He took a deep breath and could almost smell the musty smell of the gym in the jungle. He took another step against the mountain. And then another. He looked below him at Nuzu and his head spun with dizziness for just a second. He swallowed hard and looked upward toward Oko.

"Come on," Oko said. "You can do it."

Hank took another step. Rocks crumbled beneath his feet. Oko had laid down on the edge of the ledge and was reaching toward him. But to Hank, Oko's face looked distorted—and sometimes when Hank looked up, there were two images of Oko. But still Hank climbed, one foot after another, the sweat dripping from his face, the waterfall echoing in the background.

Suddenly, the light from the sun was shadowed by a dark form. Hank held on to the rope tightly and dared to look upward. When he did, he gasped.

The wings of a giant bird had blocked the sun's rays. Hank had never seen such a big bird. Its wings were twice as long as its snake-like body. It had a long neck and beak, and sharp teeth. Hank thought it looked like the pictures he had seen of a pterosaur. And it was flying down the side of the mountain, toward where he was climbing.

"Hank!" Oko shouted. "Just hang on!"

The bird swooped toward him. Hank let go of the rope with one hand. He felt himself slipping slowly downward. The bird swooped at him again. This time it hit the rope with its wings. Hank slipped downward again, ever so slightly.

"Hank!" Oko yelled from the ledge. "Get a hold of yourself! Use both hands!"

Hank regained his grip on the rope as the bird swooped down a third time. This time Hank screamed as he saw the bird's huge talons come toward him. The bird's eyes seemed to glow strangely. It called out with a hideous sound—a cross between a crow's call and dog's howl.

Suddenly the bird swooped away, toward the ground. Hank sighed with relief and looked toward where the bird was flying. It flew down toward Nuzu! Nuzu was barking wildly and running back and forth on the ground, trying to get the bird's attention. The bird swooped toward Nuzu. Nuzu ran and hid under an overhang. Then, as soon as the bird swooped away, she ran back out and got the bird's attention again.

While Nuzu distracted the bird, Hank was able to reach the ledge.

"That was close," Oko said as he helped Hank up on the ledge. "I believe we have just had an encounter with a Mokele-Mbembe. And you were so anxious to see them!"

"If I never see another Mokele-Mbembe again it will be too soon," Hank answered with a nervous laugh.

Hank and Oko were both quiet as they gazed up the steep wall they still had to climb. Hank could tell that Oko was worried—and Hank himself wondered just how long Nuzu could keep the giant bird occupied.

"Hey, what's that?" Oko asked, pointing to an indentation in the side of the mountain near the edge of the ledge. It was half-hidden by a huge boulder.

"It looks like a cave or a..."

Oko filled in the last word for Hank. "...tunnel. Maybe it leads to the valley."

"What if it doesn't?" Hank asked. "What if it leads nowhere?"

Oko looked toward the ground where the giant bird was still distracted by Nuzu. Then he looked at the side of the mountain. "I don't think we have much choice," Oko said. "Following the tunnel is our only hope."

CHAPTER SEVEN
Battle of the Giants

Hank followed Oko into the tunnel. It was darker than night inside. Hank couldn't even see the ground in front of him, but it felt soft and smelled damp. Water began dripping on his head from the roof of the tunnel.

"Are you sure this is a good idea, Oko?" Hank asked.

"I'm not sure about anything right now. Here, hold on to the end of this rope. That way we won't get separated."

Hank and Oko guided themselves through the tunnel by holding on to the rope and feeling the tunnel's slimy walls.

Suddenly, Hank felt something run over one of his feet. It didn't feel big, but it felt heavy. He let out a small scream. "Gross! Something just ran over my foot!"

"I think we've just met the inhabitants of the tunnel," Oko said. "I felt something

54

scamper over my feet, too, just a second ago. I think we're in a tunnel full of rats!"

Hank shuddered, but continued on. Every once in a while, he'd lift his feet and shake them. And every so often, he'd feel something else run lightly over his shoes.

Hank started to panic. He didn't know how much farther they had to go into the black tunnel. Maybe there was no way out of it. If they couldn't find the tunnel's exit, they'd be lost for sure. Hank felt his chest tighten. They would never find their way back out of the tunnel to the falls. They would never find his parents. And no one would ever find them.

The boys continued to feel their way in the darkness. After a few minutes, Oko let out a cry. "Hank! See the light ahead? It's the end of the tunnel. Come on!"

They picked up their pace, ignoring the scampering around their feet.

The light grew bigger the closer they came. As they turned around a bend of the tunnel, the bright sun nearly blinded them. Finally, they had come to the other end of the tunnel!

Shading their eyes from the bright sunlight, both boys surveyed the scene. They were high on the side of a mountain and below them, a lush green valley swept for miles.

As Hank looked up, a strange sensation

swept over him. The mysterious land was so beautiful it seemed to be calling him.

"Should we stop and rest a bit?" Oko asked.

"When we're this close? No way! Let's head down to the valley!" Hank said, his voice brimming with a confidence he didn't feel.

* * * * *

Hank and Oko began their journey down the mountain to the valley below. Hank was excited and scared at the same time. He didn't know what he was more frightened of— finding his parents dead, encountering another Mokele-Mbembe, or fighting off native attackers. With each step that he and Oko took, he thought about more and more things to be scared of. He shook his head. What the heck was he doing here, anyway? Was this all a bad dream? Would he wake up in the morning back in Chicago and head to the pool on his skateboard to see his friends?

But Hank knew the pain he was feeling was real. As they reached the valley, he was growing more and more tired. He stumbled, and Oko helped him to his feet. And then Oko stumbled, and Hank helped him stand up. Still, they kept walking through the steamy jungle toward the valley, toward the spot where they hoped to find their relatives.

When the sun was overhead, Hank suggested they rest and find something to eat. Oko found some nonpoisonous roots and gourds and shared them with Hank. They tasted bitter and they were difficult to chew— but Hank ate them to regain his strength.

The boys drank from a nearby stream. Oko began splashing Hank and the water felt cool against Hank's skin. Suddenly, Oko held up his hand and motioned for Hank to stop.

"I hear something," he whispered.

Hank listened, too. Now he heard something. Voices—from deep in the jungle. And they sounded as if they were coming their way.

Hank and Oko scurried under some low, long-leaved bushes by the edge of the stream and waited. From their hiding spot, they saw about a dozen natives walking single-file through the jungle. The one in the middle of the line wore a ram's-head mask.

Each native, including the one in the ram's-head mask, carried a rifle.

Hank looked through the leaves of the bush for someone he might recognize. From what Paul had told him, he figured Hudson or Powers might be with them. He squinted hard, but he didn't see Hudson among them. But there was someone he did recognize.

Walking just behind the man in the ram's-head mask was Watana, the pilot who had flown Hank and his parents from Brazzaville. Hank wondered what he was doing here.

The friends hid deeper in the bushes as the natives walked toward them. As the man in the mask and Watana passed by, Hank heard Watana say, "The Coopers sure have caused us a lot of trouble!"

Hank wondered for a second what he meant by that. But he got an answer to his question sooner than he wanted.

"The Coopers won't be a problem for long," the man in the ram's-head mask said. "They will die in an ancient Zoraba ceremony. Even though the natives aren't Zoraba, the ceremony makes them feel safe from the Mokele-Mbembe. And the Coopers deserve what they get! Nosing around where they don't belong."

Hank held his breath.

"What about the boy?" Watana asked. "Why didn't you capture him with his parents?"

"The Zoraba never sacrificed young boys. And besides, the young Cooper is no doubt dead by now."

Hank was overcome by a strangling fear. He realized he was the only one who could save his parents from the unspeakable terror.

Oko whispered to Hank, interrupting his

thoughts. "We must follow these men. They may lead us to our relatives."

Hank and Oko followed the native group, staying a safe distance behind. As they walked, the sky darkened, even though it was just mid-afternoon. Hank looked up and saw black clouds crowded together in the sky.

Hank whispered back. "We've got to follow them more closely. We don't want to lose them in the storm."

Oko nodded.

The natives moved northward just as heavy drops of rain began to fall. The man in the mask signaled to the others to leave the trail and seek shelter under some trees.

Hank and Oko ran for cover, too, just as the clouds seemed to burst open. The rain beat down. In moments, their clothes were soaked and they were standing in water up to their ankles.

The jungle became black as night as the storm worsened. Every few minutes, blinding flashes of lightning streaked down from the terrible dark sky. Ground-shaking thunder followed moments later.

From the frequent flashes of lightning and almost immediate rumbles of thunder, Hank figured the storm was just about overhead. Suddenly, after the rumble of some heavy thunder, Hank heard another sound.

"That wasn't thunder!" Hank said to Oko. Hank listened, then heard the sound again.

"It's more of a roar," Oko said.

The rain was coming down so hard, they could hardly see anything. But in the distance, ahead on the trail, they faintly saw two natives. They were running back south on the trail toward Hank and Oko.

Hank saw the man in the ram's-head mask start after the two natives. The man aimed his rifle and fired at the fleeing men. They stopped, then returned to the place where the others were taking shelter from the storm.

The roaring sound echoed again in the jungle. Then, a bolt of lightning followed, lighting up the scene.

Hank and Oko gasped! Right before their eyes, a huge creature emerged from the jungle. Hank's mouth went dry. The creature looked like pictures Hank had seen of a tyrannosaurus rex. Standing on its huge hind legs, it roared and clawed angrily at the rain clouds with its smaller front paws. When it roared, Hank could see all its knifelike teeth.

"It's a Mokele-Mbembe!" Hank said.

"It's frightened of the storm," Oko said.

"No!" Hank shouted. "Something else has scared it."

Hank sucked in a deep breath as he watched what happened next. Out of the jungle, on the other side of the trail, another creature appeared! This monster-sized creature was even bigger than the first creature. Its body was the size of a huge hippopotamus and it had a long neck and a thick tail.

Hank was so frightened he could barely stand to watch. The larger dinosaur growled at the smaller one. Lightning flashed around the creatures. The smaller dinosaur clawed the air—and then headed directly for the larger dinosaur, its teeth bared. The larger one threw its head back, and let out a horrible roar! The two began a bloody battle, tearing at each other, and clawing each other's back. Lightning flashed all around them. Blood spurted from wounds on the smaller one's back. But the larger dinosaur seemed in worse shape. It seemed to be weakening, and was taking fewer and fewer blows.

A second later, the friends saw the natives scream and scramble into the jungle. Watana fled with them, but Hank did not see the man in the mask anywhere.

"This is our chance!" Hank said to Oko. "The Mokele-Mbembe are fighting and the natives have gone. Let's run for it!"

CHAPTER EIGHT
The Lost City

Hank and Oko ran down the mountain, through the trees, as fast as they could. Hank didn't stop to look back at the Mokele-Mbembe, but somehow he knew that the larger creature was eyeing him as he ran. The roaring had stoppped—just for a second. And Hank could feel the presence of the creature against his neck. It made Hank run faster and faster into the bush.

Before Hank and Oko knew it, they were in a valley, deep in the jungle again. They stopped to catch their breath and watched as the sun broke through the clouds and shown through to the jungle floor. Everything looked incredibly green as they made their way through the dense bush.

The two boys walked silently through the jungle, the hot steam rising around them. As they walked, Hank tried not to think about the natives—they could be anywhere—around the next bend, behind the next tree, ready to aim their guns and fire.

Or there could be more Mokele-Mbembe ahead—waiting with their bared teeth for their next meal. Hank tried to remember what Oko had told him—thinking of them could only bring bad luck.

As they continued on, they saw no sign of any of the natives, the man in the ram's-head mask, or Watana. Hank figured that the natives had scattered into the jungle for safety from the dinosaurs and hadn't returned.

The two continued their walk through the valley and slowly began climbing the hill on the other side of the mountain, looking all the time for a sign of their relatives or of the Zoraba temple. The jungle was strangely quiet as they walked. Oko occasionally looked back at Hank and smiled, but Hank could tell that his mind was on the same thing—finding their relatives alive.

Hank felt hotter with each step. Once they reached the top of the next hill, they found themselves standing on a wide plateau. It was a high, flat stretch of land about half a mile wide and extending about a mile long. Surrounding the plateau was more dense jungle.

The ruins of some high stone walls stood around the outer edges of the entire plateau. In the center of the crumbling walls were the remains of some stone buildings.

Hank stopped and caught his breath. "Oko?" he asked. "Are you thinking what I'm thinking?"

"Yes. This must be the Zoraba city," Oko said, pointing to ruins of fort-like battlements that were almost hidden by thick trees and bushes. "—or what's left of it."

"Check out these things," Hank said, pointing to some carvings that lined what looked like the ruins of old steps leading upward. "They look like goats or..." Hank caught himself as a thought came to him. "They look like rams' heads..."

"It must have meant something to the Zoraba. Think, Hank. What did your parents tell you about the Zoraba? Did the rams' heads mean anything?"

"They said something about the Zoraba's god looking like a ram. And remember that Djoni said that the ram's head was a sign of power." Hank stopped and scratched his head. "Look, there's a whole row of carved stones just like them. Let's check them out."

Hank and Oko followed the steps upward. On every step, they were met by another ram's head, each one larger than the one before it. The eyes of the rams' heads seemed frozen in a cold, stony stare, as if they were pondering Hank and Oko's every move.

When they got to the top level, they stopped and looked around. There were tall white pillars overgrown with vines and foliage, most of them half fallen down. And there was a giant ram's head in the center, with what looked like an altar in front of it.

"This must have been the temple," Hank said, taking a step toward the altar.

Suddenly, his foot slid off the stone. He felt his left leg crumble beneath him and his right leg had nothing to hold on to. He flailed his arms and pulled his right leg toward him. Only then did he dare and look at where he had almost fallen. He was at the edge of a deep dark pit—and he had almost tumbled into it.

Oko had run to his side and was holding his shoulder to steady him. "Are you okay?" Oko asked.

Hank took a deep breath. "I-I guess so." Both boys looked downward into the abyss. "What is this hole doing here?"

"I do not know. But remember that this is the place that the Zoraba held their human sacrifices. Do you think the victims could have been kept there before the sacrifice began?"

Hank shuddered as he thought of his parents being sacrificed to the Mokele-Mbembe. All because of some weird project that this Jerome Hudson was involved in—some horrible project, some project that no one could know anything about. And then Hank imagined himself in the pit, waiting for his own execution. He shook himself to put the thought out of his head.

"Let's check out the other side of the altar," Oko said.

Hank swallowed hard and nodded. "Okay," he managed to say.

The friends climbed carefully over the altar to another part of the temple. As Hank's leg came down over one side, he felt something hard beneath his foot. He looked down at where he was stepping. A human skull stared back at him, its teeth bared as if it was laughing at him.

"Hey, Oko, you must be right about the sacrifices happening here. Look at this guy." Hank held up the skull to Oko and immediately had a sick feeling in his stomach. Could his parents end up like this? Could Oko's father?

"Sorry, Oko," Hank said, shaking his head. "I just wanted to laugh about something—anything. I guess this wasn't too funny..."

Just then, the friends heard a strange sound. It was like a moan, but it was echoing as if it were far away. It didn't exactly sound like a human voice—but it didn't sound like any animal that Hank knew of either.

"Hank, what do you suppose that is?"

"I don't know, but I'm tempted to bolt right out of here."

"I am frightened, too—but we must investigate. It may be a clue. It may lead us to your parents and my father."

"Or to more Mokele-Mbembe or to the Zoraba themselves!"

"We must follow it!" Oko insisted. And Hank reluctantly nodded his head.

"Listen!" Hank said. "What's that sound? It's coming from somewhere ahead, near the altar!"

Hank began walking carefully toward the altar, avoiding the pits. The moaning sounds grew a little louder and then louder still.

Now there was no doubt about where it was coming from. It was coming from one of the pits at the side of the altar.

CHAPTER NINE
The Temple of Zoraba

"Ohh..." the voice in the pit moaned weakly.

"That sounds like my father!" Oko said excitedly. Then Oko called out.

"Oko! Oko!" the voice called back. Hank couldn't understand what the man was saying, but he understood one thing—Oko's father was in pain.

"We have to help him climb out of the pit," exclaimed Oko. He looked frightened.

"Don't worry," answered Hank. "We'll help him."

Hank looked around the room. There was nothing that could help them lift the man out of the pit. But then Hank remembered the vines that he had seen just outside the temple. They might help pull Oko's father out of the pit.

"I'll be right back," Hank said to Oko.

Hank ran out of the room and then out of

the temple. Outside, he began pulling down long lengths of vine that seemed to hang everywhere. Dragging half a dozen yards of the vine after him, he rushed back to the pit.

"Try this, Oko!" Hank said, smiling.

Oko tossed one end of the vine down into the hole. He and Hank held on to the other end.

After a few minutes, the voice called back.

"He's ready," said Oko. "Let's pull him up. But be careful, Hank. He thinks his leg might be broken."

Hank and Oko pulled on the line while Oko's father eased himself upward. It took a long time. Sweat beaded on Hank's brow. But they pulled and pulled, using their last bit of strength.

Finally, Hank could see the figure of Oko's father near the top of the pit. He climbed up and stared at Hank and Oko for a second, as if in disbelief. Then Oko and his father fell into each other's arms. Hank felt tears in his eyes as Oko sobbed with happiness.

Oko's father sat down at the edge of the pit and took a few deep breaths. Hank tried not to be impatient. He knew that the man needed to gather his strength. But his chest was growing tight again. He was more worried than ever. Time was passing much too quickly.

And now that Oko had found his father, he had to find his own parents—and quickly. He hoped Oko's father might have a clue to where his parents were.

"Father," said Oko in English. "This is Hank, a friend who has made a long journey with me. He is searching for his parents. They were also kidnapped."

"Tell me all you know, Mr..."

"Call me Kari."

"Please help me, Kari," Hank said, urgently. "I've just got to find my parents."

"Two weeks ago, I was kidnapped by natives." Kari explained. "One of them wore a ram's-head mask."

"The Zoraba?" Hank asked.

"I don't think that they were the Zoraba. But I think that they were masquerading as the Zoraba. They have been kidnapping natives to work on a project in the swamp in the valley. They have set up a camp there. A man named Jerome Hudson is at the center of it all."

"I knew it!" Hank said to himself. "I knew that Hudson was in the middle of this somehow."

"What kind of project?" Oko asked.

"That I do not know. I didn't get close enough to find out. I tried to escape, and, as

I did, I hurt my leg. They threw me in the pit to die. They said I would be of no use as a slave. They said that I could not haul their precious cargo. And then they laughed. I do not know what the cargo is—or why they are carrying it into the jungle."

"Have you seen a woman who looks like she might be my mother?" Hank asked Oko's father.

Kari shook his head that he hadn't. "Was she taken by the man in the mask?" Kari asked.

"Yes," Hank answered. "Do you know who he is?"

"No, he hides behind his mask. And I only heard him speak from far down in the pit," Kari said. Kari eased himself upward as he spoke and tried to stand, but his left leg gave way under him.

"I'm afraid my leg is too weak to walk on. Oko, you and your friend must find our people and Hank's parents on your own," Kari said.

"I cannot leave you alone, Father," Oko said.

"Do not worry. I will hide nearby. Go, my son. Find the camp. But be very careful. The man in the mask is very dangerous."

Hank watched as Oko looked into his father's eyes.

"Look, Oko," Hank said reluctantly. "Why

71

don't you and your dad head back to your village? I can manage on my own."

Oko considered Hank's words.

"No, I mean it," Hank said. "My parents are around here someplace—they're very close. I can feel it."

"Hank, you have come this far with me," Oko said. "I cannot leave you now."

"And besides," Kari said. "They are holding many of our people captive. You must go—you must hurry, before more lives are lost."

Oko nodded his head. "He is right, Hank. And besides, we are brothers, right?"

"Right!" Hank said, relieved that Oko was going with him.

The boys helped Kari into a small cave in a cliff at the side of the temple. The small cave was covered with vines and leaves. Hank and Oko left him there, confident that he would not be found. But as they left, Hank had a nagging fear in his mind about the Mokele-Mbembe. They were the real danger to Kari now.

The two boys made their way through the dense jungle, following in the direction that Kari had pointed out. At times, the brush was so dense that it was difficult to get their bearings—but they headed on anyway, guessing which way to go. According to Kari, they were to head toward the gorge, and then east, where they would find the camp.

Hank lost track of how long they had walked. The hours melted into each other. Hank remembered that he had just one more night to find his parents. The full moon was only 24 hours away.

Hank wondered how he would rescue his parents if he did find them. He'd have to find some way to get them to safety—but how?

The farther they walked toward the valley, the hotter it became, even though the sun began to set on the horizon. Steam rose from the jungle in a thick green mist. Hank found it harder and harder to breathe.

At last, they reached the ridge that surrounded the valley. They hid in some bushes and looked down into the valley. Hank was amazed. The wide valley was greener and wilder than anything he had ever seen. Some of the valley lay under water. Gigantic weeds and trees grew on the swampy land.

Oko nudged Hank and brought his fingers to his lips. Then he pointed to one side of the valley. Hank looked in the direction of Oko's finger and saw what he had discovered.

A group of natives were working in the shallow water of one of the swamps. They seemed to be digging in the mud.

Before Hank and Oko could move closer, the sun began to set behind the trees. A great shadow fell over the valley.

In the growing darkness, some lights began to shine. Natives carrying rifles were starting to light torches. In the glow of the torches, Hank and Oko watched as the men holding the rifles began assembling the diggers into a single line. Then the torch-carriers guided the diggers away from the swamp.

"It looks like they're taking them back to the camp for the night," Hank whispered.

Hank and Oko watched the torches move like a glowing snake up the trail. Just as the last of the native slaves headed up the trail, they heard a rumbling sound overhead.

"It sounds like the cargo plane," Oko said, looking up at the sky.

They stood in silence and listened. Soon the plane's lights cut through the dark sky. It flew lower than Hank had ever seen it before—barely clearing the treetops.

The plane flew over the valley. Then it began to circle over the swamps. Suddenly, Hank saw something drop from the plane and land in the swamp. Then the plane flew south.

"What do you think that was?" Hank whispered to Oko.

"I don't know," Oko whispered back.

"What do you think we should do now?" Hank asked, his voice rising above a whisper.

Oko looked blankly back at him. Neither of the boys knew what to do next.

Oko spoke first. "Look, Hank," he said. "We don't have a chance of helping the prisoners escape while they're in the camp. And we don't see your parents here. Maybe we should just camp out here and we can help them in the morning when they return to the valley. That might give us time to think of a way to rescue them."

Hank shook his head. "It's risky, I know, but we've got to check out the camp tonight. We don't have much time." Hank was surprised by the confidence in his voice. He didn't feel confident. He felt afraid. "Maybe I can find my mother and father there."

Hank and Oko had a hard time staying on the trail in the dark. And all the time Hank was walking, he sensed something or someone was following him—watching him.

He wondered if it was a native or maybe even the man in the mask. He hadn't seen him with the other natives. Maybe it was a Mokele-Mbembe, watching him and waiting for the right moment to pounce on him.

But Hank and Oko safely reached the outskirts of the camp. They didn't see any

75

torchlight or anyone walking around. They only heard the chattering of some monkeys climbing the vines covering the buildings.

They crept toward the camp, keeping close to the buildings. They began to hear chanting. The noise seemed to be coming from a campfire in the middle of the camp.

Fears began to race through Hank's mind. Maybe the guards were starting one of the Zoraba's ancient ceremonies. Maybe they were about to make a sacrifice. What if they were about to sacrifice his parents?

Suddenly, Hank's blood ran cold. He saw a native with a torch lighting the way for the man in the ram's-head mask. They headed to the center of the camp, toward the campfire, where a huge stone slab stood. The drums and chanting grew louder and faster.

The friends were about to leave their hiding place when they saw torchlights. Two guards were shoving a prisoner toward the stone slab. The man's hands were tied and he tried to resist. But the guards held him by the arms and forced him along.

Hank couldn't see who the victim was, so he left the hiding place to get a closer look. He inched nearer to the stone slab. His heart sank to his stomach when he recognized the man who was about to be sacrificed!

CHAPTER TEN
On the Brink

The victim was Hank's father!

Hank watched as the two guards with torches pushed his father toward the center of the fire circle. Then he scampered back to the hiding place.

Hank looked at Oko. Oko didn't need to ask any questions.

"My father," Hank whispered.

Hank had to think fast. If he wanted to free his father, he had to do it now, before the actual ceremony began. Once it started, all eyes would be on the center of the circle. It would be too late.

Hank gestured to Oko and they left their hiding place and crept toward the base of the steps. It was covered with vines. Hank pulled down handfuls of the thick vine.

He saw the guards move his father toward the chanting tribe.

Hank knew he'd have to surprise the men holding his father. "Just follow my lead," Hank whispered to Oko. He took a deep breath, then let out a loud, terrible cry.

The two guards stopped on the stairs. Hank rushed forward and threw the monkey rope at them. Oko followed, throwing more vines.

Both guards dropped their torches. As they tried to free themselves from the tangled vines, Hank rushed to free his father.

"It's me, Dad, Hank!" he said, untying his father's hands.

"Hank, how did you get here?" Jeff Cooper asked in astonishment.

"There's no time to explain now, Dad," Hank said. "Let's get out of here!"

Just then, the man in the ram's-head mask appeared from out of the crowd. In a loud voice he shouted to a guard. He pointed at Hank. But Oko tossed a vine at the guard's feet. He tripped over the vine and fell down the stone stairs.

The three of them ran into the dark jungle.

"They'll send a search party after us," Jeff Cooper said. "But they'll have a hard time finding us in the jungle." He nodded toward Oko. "Good thinking, son!" he said to Oko.

"Dad," Hank broke in. "This is my friend, Oko. He is from a tribe in the village—or what's left of it. Members of his village are being kidnapped to be slaves. We have found his father—he was left to die in a pit in the temple. But the rest of his tribe are still working as slaves."

"We'll find them, son—we'll find out what's going on." Jeff Cooper said, his voice full of urgency. "And we'll find your mother, too, Hank."

"What happened to her, Dad?"

"I don't know," his father said. "I haven't seen her for two days. But I think she's still alive. I was to be sacrificed tonight. They were saving her for the full moon—tomorrow. They said that taking our lives would appease the Mokele-Mbembe—if they even exist."

"They exist, all right, Dad. Haven't you seen them?"

"No. I've only heard the stories. Have you?"

Hank looked at Oko. "Yeah, we've seen them. But they aren't exactly dinosaurs— more like giant lizards, as if nature went crazy or something," Hank said.

Jeff shook his head. "This is a mystery of nature, a terrible mystery. Something's wrong in the valley," he added. "Very wrong."

The three were silent for a moment as they made their way through the bush. Every once in a while, Hank's father would ruffle his son's hair, and nudge him gently on his shoulders. Hank was glad to see his dad—but he still felt very anxious about his mom.

Suddenly, they heard a roaring overhead.

"It sounds like a chopper," Hank said.

"What would a helicopter be doing flying over the mountain?" Jeff asked.

"Remember what Watana said?" Hank asked. "He told us in the plane that it was too dangerous for helicopters to land here. It's supposed to be too windy. Funny, but I haven't noticed it's especially windy up here."

"The helicopter's heading north," Jeff observed.

"Toward the valley," Hank said. "Let's go see if it lands there."

Hank's father led the way back up the trail toward the valley just as the sun was coming over the horizon. Hank and Oko followed.

Before they reached the valley, they heard sounds coming from back in the jungle. They hid in some bushes and watched as the natives who had been held prisoner in the temple were walked again to the marshes to work.

They watched as the chopper landed. The engine shut down and the pilot stepped out.

"It's Watana!" Hank said.

"Who is he helping out of the chopper?" his father asked.

An important-looking man in a tan suit, with thick, gray hair, stepped out next.

"I've never seen him before," Hank said. "I'll bet he's Grayson Powers, the man Paul told me about. And look! There's Jerome Hudson!"

Hudson came out of the jungle and approached the helicopter. When the man in the tan suit saw him, he waved in a friendly manner and called to him. Hudson went up and shook the man's hand, then began talking to him.

"That man must have hired Hudson to oversee the natives," Hank's father whispered.

Hank heard some voices coming up the trail from the direction of the swamp.

"Look! Here comes the man in the ram's-head mask," Hank said.

He and his father watched as the masked native led the procession of slaves and guards into the valley where the helicopter stood. They heard Grayson Powers yell.

"Get rid of them!" Powers said. "We can't take any chances now!"

Hank whispered to his father, "Get rid of the slaves, or us?"

"Probably us," Jeff said. "But that isn't going to be as easy as Powers thinks."

Oko motioned for them to be quiet. They were much too close—and if they were caught it meant certain death. They had to be absolutely silent. Hank held his breath as Hudson and Powers began arguing.

"I've had enough, Mr. Powers," Hudson said. "I wasn't expecting to kill anyone."

"What does it matter if a few natives are killed because they're sick or are too lazy to work?" Powers asked Hudson. "Their deaths can always be blamed on the Mokele-Mbembes. The natives are stupid enough to believe in those creatures."

"But there are dinosaurs up here!" Hudson insisted. "One chased me yesterday."

"Don't be ridiculous," Powers snapped at Hudson. "We spread the rumor about the Mokele-Mbembes, didn't we, Watana? It makes our work up here easier. Talk of dinosaurs living up here keeps people away. And it scares the natives so they'll stay in line and work for us. Besides, Hudson, you're getting paid enough not to care about some overgrown lizards or a few natives being killed."

"I thought I could do just about anything for the kind of money you're paying me," Hudson said. "But this has gone too far. I'm not going to be involved in murdering Julie Cooper—or the rest of her family." Hank gasped and looked at his father, whose face had turned sheet-white.

"I'm out of the deal," Hudson was continuing. "I'm going back to London."

"You're in too deep to get out now," Powers said to Hudson. "You leave me no alternative." He nodded to Watana.

The pilot took a gun out of an inside pocket. He smiled, aiming it at Hudson.

"You'll do what Mr. Powers says or you'll end up in the sacrifice pit!" Watana told Hudson. Hudson stared for a moment at the ugly barrel of Watana's gun. Then he backed away and hung his head.

"You both have work to do," Powers told them. "It shouldn't take you long to find Cooper and his son. Get rid of them, and Mrs. Cooper. I had hoped to spare the boy—that's why I left him when we kidnapped his parents. But he has proved to be much too resourceful. Once they're all out of the way, we'll have nothing to worry about."

Powers then spoke to the man in the mask.

"You keep these natives under control or I'll find someone else to wear that mask," Powers threatened. "I gave you the mask and I can take it away. If you are going to behave as the ancient Zoraba, you must have control. Do you understand me?"

The masked native nodded that he did, but said nothing. He ordered his guards to push the slaves down to the swamp.

Watana and Hudson walked back toward the temple. Powers returned to the helicopter and sat in its shade.

"So Powers is behind everything up here," Jeff Cooper whispered. "And we don't know what work the slaves are put to. But you can bet it's something that puts a lot of money in Powers' pockets."

The group turned and headed through the jungle toward the temple. On the crest of a ridge, they turned to see Watana and Hudson in the distance.

"Look!" Hank cried. "They've got company."

Jeff Cooper saw what Hank meant. Two huge Mokele-Mbembes had wandered out of the jungle and spotted Watana, Hudson, and the guards. The dinosaurs charged them. The guards fled into the jungle. Their frightened screams floated on the hot air of the valley.

The three of them turned away and continued in the direction of the temple. Oko headed toward the cave where his father was still hiding. Hank and his father began searching the temple, hoping to find Julie Cooper. They called softly down into the pits. They looked behind each pillar. But they saw nothing.

Oko had left his father and was searching

in the rear of the temple. Suddenly, he called, "Over here!"

Hank and his father followed the sound of Oko's voice. When they caught up to Oko, he lead them through a passageway that they had not seen before. They had to crouch underneath arches to get through. After awhile, they found themselves in a great throne room, the inner sanctum of the temple.

Just then, they heard a soft voice from a dark corner.

"Over here!" the voice said.

Hank ran to his mother as soon as he saw her. She was tied to some rings on the wall. Hank and his father undid the knots of the ropes that held her to the rings. She fell to the floor in exhaustion.

"MOM!" Hank said. "I thought we'd never see you again!" Tears were welling up in Hank's eyes as he spoke. He noticed that his father's eyes were misty, too.

"I thought I would die in this horrible place!" she said. "I couldn't bear it!"

"We've got to get out of here!" Jeff said. "Someone could find us here any minute."

But just then, Hank heard a scream outside the building. When he ran out, he found himself staring right into the barrel of a rifle.

CHAPTER ELEVEN
The Natives' Revenge

The man behind the rifle was Watana. Jerome Hudson was standing beside him. When Hank's father and mother came out, Hudson held his rifle on them.

"Your time has come," Watana said. "Go now. Up the temple steps. You will all be sacrificed NOW. We will not wait for the Zoraba and the official ceremony. We will simply find a native for them to sacrifice instead."

He began to laugh an evil laugh. Hank noticed that Hudson seemed more scared than ever.

It was the end, and Hank knew it. And after they had come this far. He looked at his father and his mother. He would never get back to Chicago. He would never see the Cubs play again or go to the pool with his friends. He tried to think of a plan as they walked toward the base of the temple. But Hank couldn't think straight. The guards began pushing them up the big stone steps. He felt the cold steel of Watana's rifle in his back.

"What's that noise?" Hudson asked, turning to look behind him.

Hank and his parents looked, too. Hank gasped. What they saw gave them new hope.

Dozens of natives began flooding into the ancient Zoraba city. They waved spears over their heads and yelled. Leading the crowd was someone Hank recognized. It was Paul—Paul Ruffington.

And beside Paul was a sight even more bizarre! It was Nuzu! And next to Paul ran Oko, followed by the band of angry natives.

"Put down your rifles," Paul said, approaching Watana and Hudson. "This is your last stand, Hudson. I have waited a long time for this day—to finally put you and your team of criminals out of business before you destroy all of Africa!"

Watana and Hudson handed over their rifles to Hank's father. He handed one to Julie. The crowd of angry natives gave up a roar, and several natives tied the men up.

Then Paul approached Hank and his parents.

"Paul!" Hank said. "I thought you were..."

"You thought I was dead? Ah, you underestimate the Aussie will to survive."

"But the Gates of Terror...I saw your hat floating. And the river was full of crocodiles!"

"I can't explain exactly what happened. All I know is I washed up down river somewhere. When I came to, this dog here was licking my face. And then he led me over the mountains and, eventually, to this valley."

"Oko, your dog is incredible!" Hank said, embracing his friend. But how did you two climb the waterfall?" Hank asked.

"We didn't. Nuzu seemed to know a different way. She took me around the waterfall to a path in the back."

Hank just shook his head in disbelief.

"Now we have to get Grayson Powers," Jeff Cooper said.

He and Hank led the way. The natives followed, holding rifles and spears on Hudson and Watana. They headed back up the trail to where Powers was waiting in the helicopter.

"He's probably armed, so we have to be careful," Jeff Cooper told the others. "When he sees we're in control of the situation, he may not give up without trying something."

When they got close to the helicopter, Powers saw them coming. He called to the man in the ram's-head mask for help.

The masked native came up from the swamps with his guards. But when they turned their backs on their prisoners for a moment, the natives they were guarding jumped them. In only seconds, the slaves had overpowered their masters.

Seeing he was without any protection, Powers got into the pilot's seat of the chopper. Frantically, he began trying to work the control panel.

"He doesn't know how to fly it," Watana said.

"Look! He's getting it off the ground!" Hank yelled.

One of the natives ran toward the helicopter and fired his rifle at it. But the shot was wild and missed the chopper.

"He's getting away!" Watana said.

"No! Look!" someone shouted.

Something flew out of the swamp and over their heads. It was a giant bird, flapping its wings as it headed for the helicopter!

Hank thought it looked like the giant-winged bird that had attacked him on the cliff. Everyone in the crowd held their breath as the huge, winged dinosaur flew up to challenge the mechanical bird that was rising into the sunlit sky.

CHAPTER TWELVE
Pieces of the Puzzle

Everyone watched in amazement as the giant bird forced Powers' helicopter back down to the ground. Then the bird began pecking at the metal roof of the chopper. Inside, Powers' face was paralyzed with terror. Hank stared, unable to move, at the incredible sight—a living dinosaur attacking a helicopter! Then, suddenly, the giant bird flew off into the sky.

Jeff Cooper held his rifle on the industrialist as Powers climbed out of the chopper.

"I don't know what this is all about," Powers said. "You have no right to point a rifle at me. This was *their* scheme, not mine," he said, pointing to Hudson and Watana. "They told me to come here. They said they had a business proposition for me. I don't know what they've been doing up here, and I demand that you let me go!"

Then he looked up to see Paul Ruffington standing there and shook his head. "You, again! How dare you ruin another—" Powers caught himself before he could go any further.

"Ruin another what?" Paul spat angrily. "It is *you* who is ruining the jungle, destroying all that nature put there. What's next for you? The rain forests?"

"I-I am ruining nothing!" Powers said.

"Oh, yeah? What is this secret project in the valley, and what are you burying there?"

"You'll never know!" Powers spat back.

As Paul spoke, Hank eyed Hudson. His face was full of sad creases. He looked like a defeated man. He nudged his father.

"Ruffington!" Jeff Cooper shouted. "I believe Hudson here has something to say, don't you, Hudson?"

"Well, I...I..."

"If you want us to ask the authorities to go easy on you, you'd better tell us exactly what is going on," Hank told Hudson.

"Powers is behind it all," Hudson said, finally breaking down. "For over a year, they've been burying toxic waste up here."

"I suspected as much!" Paul said. "Grayson never could clean up after himself. Could this have anything to do with any of your businesses, Grayson? You must be involved in 40

91

or 50 businesses that produce toxic waste."

"Then that was what the planes were used for. They must have been carrying the toxic waste to the valley to be dumped," Hank said. "And Grayson's men kidnapped the natives to force them to bury it!"

The industrialist said nothing. He only lowered his head silently.

"Is Hank right, Jerome?" Jeff asked Hudson.

"Yes," Hudson replied. "Powers thought no one would know he was polluting the jungle."

"But you did not count on the mutations, did you?" Paul asked.

"The mutations?" Powers asked, confused. "W-what are you talking about?"

"The Mokele-Mbembe. The animals and birds we've seen that look like dinosaurs. They're really just lizards and birds—horribly mutated lizards and birds that have grown to giant size because of the toxic pollution in the valley. They've been changed into monsters because of the poison *you* dumped here! I don't know what the future has in store for the natives that you forced to work on your project. But it cannot be pleasant! I fear for what may happen to them!"

Hank shuddered with horror when he thought of what had happened to the animals of the poisoned swamp. Would something terrible happen to the innocent natives who had slaved in the swamp, too?

"Nor will your future be pleasant, once the authorities hear of this," Jeff Cooper added. "It will take years—maybe centuries for this part of the jungle to recover."

"We've got to get everyone out of the valley to allow the land to heal and to prevent further damage." Paul said. "It's time to leave. We'll take these prisoners back down the mountain to the authorities. And the natives..."

Hank looked at Oko.

"They will need to leave this place, too. Someday, when the land is back to its natural state, they can return. Now, they must live in Mzadi, far from danger," Paul finished.

"What about the man in the ram's-head mask?" Jeff Cooper asked.

"Here he is!" cried Kari. "The others have tied him up."

Oko and his father brought the native in the mask forward. Kari began to lift the mask off the man's face.

"Tongo!" Kari exclaimed.

Hank remembered the cruel face of Djoni's son.

"So you could not wait to become priest of your own tribe," Kari told the man. "You would be a shaman of the Zoraba and the valley of the Mokele-Mbembe—even if it meant enslaving your own people. It is *you* who has held our tribe in its terrible slavery!"

"Someone else, not Tongo, will lead us, after Djoni passes on to paradise," Oko's father said. "Perhaps Oko will be the chosen one. He has proven his bravery."

The natives cheered and held up their spears. Oko smiled shyly.

It was a long, hot trip through the jungle back over the mountains to Mzadi. Powers, Watana, Hudson, and Tongo were carefully guarded until the police came several days later. Everyone watched as the criminals were taken away to be tried for their crimes.

Djoni shook his head sadly as his son was taken away. Then he turned to his people and announced that there would be a festival.

"We will honor our guests, the Coopers and Paul Ruffington," Djoni told his people. "And offer thanks that our tribesmen have returned safely. We will mourn those who lost their lives in the valley of terror because of a rich man's greed and a foolish son's ambition."

Hank spent his last morning in the Congo saying good-bye to Oko and Nuzu. Around noon, he and his parents were ready to leave for Brazzaville where they would catch an airliner that would take them home.

Hank turned to Oko. "You know, Oko, if you practice basketball, maybe you'll win a scholarship to the school in Brazzaville. Then maybe you can visit me in the states!"

"There is a first time for everything," Oko said. Hank laughed and hugged his friend.

Later, Hank was flying over the Congo on the way back to Brazzaville. He looked at the high Zoraba Mountains.

"I hope that you will be able to come back someday," his father told him. "I hope that the Zoraba Valley will survive and that you and your children can explore the lost city of Zoraba."

In his heart, Hank knew that someday, somehow, he would return. Perhaps Oko would be shaman then, and have a child of his own. And, with their children, he and Oko would explore the wilderness—a new wilderness, a new land just beginning to heal.

He took a deep sigh and reclined. He closed his eyes and dreamed of dinosaurs, tunnels full of rats, men in ram's-head masks, of his friend, Oko, and of seeing the Chicago Cubs play. But the dream that made him most happy, was the dream of new life in the land over the mountain, a new and different world for his children and for Oko's children.

About the Author

WALTER OLEKSY is a former reporter for the *Chicago Tribune* and a former editor of three travel magazines. He now writes books full-time. Among his books for adults are a cookbook, a true adventure story of a canoeing trip, and a history of the one-room schoolhouse. He has written a biography of Soviet leader Mikhail Gorbachev for young readers. His first book for Willowisp Press, *The Dagger of Death,* introduces Hank and his parents and takes them to the wild jungles of South America.

He enjoys camping, wilderness canoeing, and playing Frisbee with his dog. He lives in Evanston, Illinois.